Bernice
Blackcurrant

Alice Apple

Peter
Potato

Grace Grape

Wee Willie
Water Melon

The Garden Gang
Stories and pictures by Jayne Fisher

Other Garden Gang stories

Series 793

Gertrude Gooseberry

Ladybird Books Loughborough

Gertrude Gooseberry
was prim and
very, very clever.
She had come to stay
in a sweet little cottage
in Blackberry Dell
for a holiday.
She brought
lots of books
to keep her occupied.
Miss Gertrude
did not like to be idle
even when she was
on holiday.
"Idle hands,"
she said, "get up to
mischief."

4

She was quite right.
The Chive and
Blackberry children
were already
getting into mischief.
They were idle and bored.
You see, the
kindly old schoolmaster,
Tobias Turnip,
had had rather a
nasty accident
whilst taking the
school-children
on a nature walk.
He had slipped
on a twig and
broken his leg.

There was no one else
to take his place
in the school.
The Blackberry
and Chive children
became more mischievous,
and their poor parents
became more worried.
What could they do?
The Garden Gang all had
a meeting to see what
could be done.
It was Mark Marrow
who suggested that
they should go to visit
Gertrude Gooseberry
to see if she could help.

9

The next morning
Mark Marrow, Oliver Onion
and Roger Radish set off
up the hill to
Gertrude's cottage.
It was a lovely day and
Gertrude Gooseberry
was reading
in the shade of
a lilac tree.
"Good morning," she said.
"Can I help you?"
They looked at
each other shyly.
Then Oliver Onion
blurted out
the whole story.

"I will need to
think for a while,"
Gertrude said,
after Oliver had finished
his unhappy tale.
"But first I will make
a nice cup of tea.
Sit down, all of you."
They sat down quickly,
like three
naughty children,
and waited for
the tea to arrive.

It was not long
before Miss Gertrude
reappeared with a tray,
on which was a
steaming pot of tea
and a great pile of hot,
buttered toast.
She poured the tea
and handed round
the toast.
It was delicious,
and the three friends
looked at Gertrude
admiringly.

"Well, now," she said,
when they had all
finished eating,
"about these
naughty children.
Would you like me
to teach them?
It would be a
pleasure to me
and it would help you
out of your difficulties."

The three friends
were so delighted
that at first
they were speechless.
It was Mark Marrow
who eventually managed
to stammer,
"Thank you so much.
How kind of you.
Thank you very much.
Thank you,
we are so pleased.
Thank you,
we are delighted.
Thank you, er . . .
thank you."

19

"I will start immediately,"
Gertrude said, and
she marched down the hill
to the school.
Here, the ink-throwing,
rubber-bouncing,
milk-spilling,
scribble-writing,
paper-tearing,
book-throwing,
chair-banging,
ruler-wobbling,
fighting children
were leaping around
the classroom,
quite unaware
of her approach.

21

Five minutes later
you could have heard
a pin drop in school.
In ten more minutes
the mess had been
cleared up,
the children were
washed and neat,
and school
had begun.

The children were
so interested
in the work
Gertrude Gooseberry
gave them,
that they stopped
being mischievous
and became
very studious.
They all worked hard
and begged her
to stay for ever.
She agreed,
and Tobias Turnip . . .

retired
happily!

Belinda Blackcurrant

Belinda Blackcurrant
was a sweet little thing.
Everybody liked her.
She always had
a happy, smiling face.
But one thing
worried her father
and mother.
There was no one
in the garden
of her own age
and they felt
that sometimes Belinda
seemed a little lonely,
although she
never complained.

Belinda was not only
sweet and happy
but she was
very clever and helpful.
She had lots of uncles
and aunts,
quite a number
of older cousins
and hundreds
of baby cousins
and often
went to help them
if they were
busy or ill.

One day,
Belinda went to visit
her cousin Beatrice,
only to find her
in bed
with a heavy cold.
She quickly
cleaned the house,
tidied Beatrice's bed,
made her
lots of hot drinks
and by the time
she had to leave
in the evening
Beatrice was sitting up
in her little bed
feeling very much better.

Another time,
when Belinda's mother
had to go out
for the day
she made some
shortbread, flapjacks,
iced buns, a fruit flan,
chocolate cake
and some sausage rolls.
Then,
when she had finished,
she carefully washed
each spoon and bowl,
leaving the kitchen
as clean and bright
as a new pin.

When her mother
got home,
feeling very tired,
she was delighted
to see all the baking
that Belinda
had done for her.
Instead of having
to spend the rest
of the afternoon
working in her kitchen,
she was able
to sit quietly
by the fireside
with her feet up,
drinking a nice
cup of tea.

Belinda was very good
at looking after
children too.
She often took
her young cousins
to the park.
She bought them
ice-creams,
and sometimes crisps,
and if they were
very, very good,
she would take them
for a ride
on a large boat
round and round
the boating pool.

39

All this time,
Belinda was still lonely.
She would have liked
a little house
of her own,
because she was
a very good housekeeper.
But her mother
and father
did not like the idea
of her living alone
and wished and wished
that she could find
a little friend.

Then it happened –
one night the garden
was struck by
a terrible thunderstorm.
Rain and wind
lashed the plants
and trees
in the garden.
As Belinda stood there
with her hands
over her ears,
suddenly, over the wall
from the next door garden
was blown the most
handsome blackcurrant
she had ever seen.
His name was Bernard.

43

It was love
at first sight.
They looked at each other
for many minutes
and then went off
hand in hand
to see Belinda's parents
who were delighted
that at last Belinda
had found a friend.
Bernard and Belinda
decided to be married
the very next week,
and everyone
was overjoyed.

Friends and neighbours
built Belinda's
dream cottage in
the corner of the garden.
The Church
was decorated
with beautiful flowers
and the choir chives
practised the
wedding hymns
over and over again
just to make sure
that everything would be
perfect for Bernard
and Belinda's wedding.

47

At last
the great day dawned.
The sun shone,
the birds sang
and the sky
was bright blue.
The Church was full
of delighted people
and the choir chives
sang better than they
had ever done before.
When the smiling couple
at last appeared
in the church doorway,
everyone knew
that Bernard and Belinda
would live . . .

happily ever after!

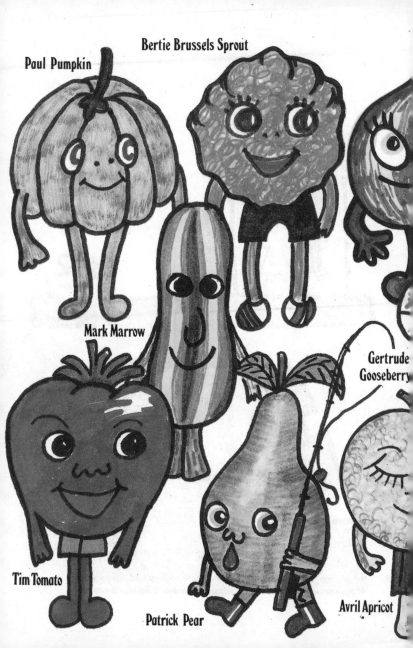